# The Author with the Fancy Purple Pen

Writing Center

Paper

Picture file

Story Starters

Books about writing

Miss Lucy had a student.
Her name was Jenny White.
She sat her at the table
to see if she could write.

3

Jenny watched a spider.
She watched a little bird.

4

She fell asleep. She took a nap.
She did not write one word!

Miss Lucy called the principal.
She called her teacher friend.

Miss Lucy called the author
with the fancy purple pen!

In came the principal.
In came the friend.

In came the author
with the fancy purple pen.

9

"Write . . ." said the principal.
"Every day," said the friend.

". . . in a journal!" said the author
with the fancy purple pen.

Out went the principal.
Out went the friend.

Out went the author
with the fancy purple pen.

Miss Lucy had a student.
Her name was Jenny White.
She used her journal every day,
and Jenny learned to write!

**1** Write a little each day in your journal. Write about things you notice around you or special things that are going on. Write about your pet, your family, your friends—your world!

**2** Look through your journal when you need an idea for a story or poem.